Put Beginning Readers on the Right Track with
ALL ABOARD READING™

The All Aboard Reading series is especially for beginning readers. Written by noted authors and illustrated in full color, these are books that children really and truly *want* to read—books to excite their imagination, tickle their funny bone, expand their interests, and support their feelings. With four different reading levels, All Aboard Reading lets you choose which books are most appropriate for your children and their growing abilities.

Picture Readers—for Ages 3 to 6
Picture Readers have super-simple texts with many nouns appearing as rebus pictures. At the end of each book are 24 flash cards—on one side is the rebus picture; on the other side is the written-out word.

Level 1—for Preschool through First Grade Children
Level 1 books have very few lines per page, very large type, easy words, lots of repetition, and pictures with visual "cues" to help children figure out the words on the page.

Level 2—for First Grade to Third Grade Children
Level 2 books are printed in slightly smaller type than Level 1 books. The stories are more complex, but there is still lots of repetition in the text and many pictures. The sentences are quite simple and are broken up into short lines to make reading easier.

Level 3—for Second Grade through Third Grade Children
Level 3 books have considerably longer texts, use harder words and more complicated sentences.

All Aboard for happy reading!

For Joe and Ann, with love—P.B.D.

To Dr. Mark, for just Being There—
Love from M.S.

Special thanks to John Garwood, M.D., Pediatrician, Mt. Sinai Hospital, New York, NY.

Library of Congress Cataloging-in-Publication Data

Demuth, Patricia.
    Achoo! : all about colds / Patricia Brennan Demuth ; illustrations
by Maggie Smith.
      p.   cm.
    Summary: Explains how a person catches a cold, how the body fights
the germs, and how other people can take precautions against getting
another's cold.
    1. Cold (Disease)—Juvenile literature. [1. Cold (Disease)
2. Diseases.] I. Smith, Maggie, 1965-   ill. II. Title.
  RF361.D45 1997
  616.2'05—dc20

96-31898
CIP
AC

ISBN 0-448-41348-5 (GB) A B C D E F G H I J

ISBN 0-448-41347-7 (pbk.) A B C D E F G H I J

ALL
ABOARD
READING™

**Level 1
Preschool-Grade 1**

ACHOO!

ALL ABOUT COLDS

**By Patricia Brennan Demuth
Illustrated by Maggie Smith**

Grosset & Dunlap • New York

Today
Sam is playing baseball.
He is at second base.
Achoo!
Oh no!
Sam does not catch the ball.

But he has caught a cold.

He sneezes some more.

His throat hurts.

His nose is running.

Sam feels sick.

Sam was feeling fine last week.

So how did he catch the cold?

It was cold one day.

Sam played outside.

Did the cold make Sam sick?

No.

Nobody gets a cold

from <u>being</u> cold.

9

Sam got his cold at school
a few days ago.
His friend Sara had a cold.

Achoo!

Sara sneezed.

Tiny germs flew out.

Billy picked up some of them.

But he did not catch Sara's cold.

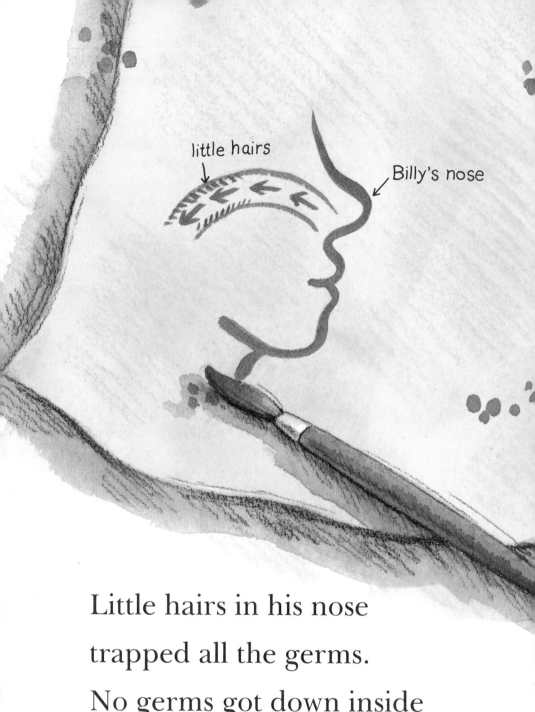

little hairs

Billy's nose

Little hairs in his nose
trapped all the germs.
No germs got down inside
Billy's body.

13

Billy was lucky.

Sam was not.

Sara sneezed again.

Some cold germs

got past Sam's nose.

They went down his throat.

They started to make

more germs.

At first, there were just a few.

Then thousands.

Then millions!

Will the germs take over

Sam's body?

Not a chance.

Sam's body can fight back.

Everyone's body is made of tiny parts called cells.

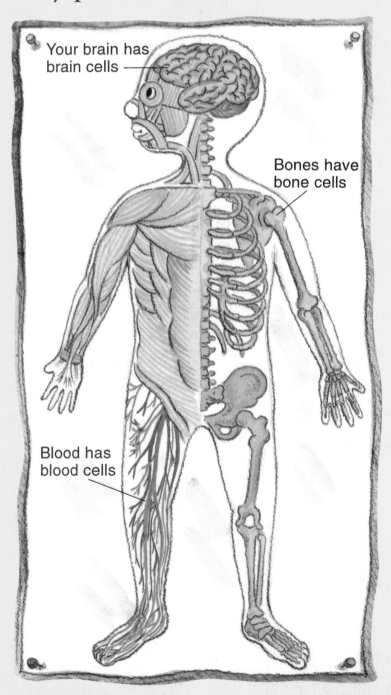

Your brain has brain cells

Bones have bone cells

Blood has blood cells

There are brain cells
and bone cells and blood cells.
Some blood cells
can fight germs.
Now that Sam has a cold,
these fighter cells get busy.
Some grab the germs.
Others gobble them up.
Sam's body makes
more and more
fighter cells.
They kill more and
more germs.
Does this make Sam feel better?
No! Not right away.

By the day of the game,
Sam feels sick.
He is happy to go home.

The germs that made Sam sick
are very small.
Millions of them can fit
on the dot of this "i."
But they can cause big trouble.
Achoo! ACHOO!
Sam's nose keeps running.
And now his throat really hurts.

Later Sam puts on his pj's.

He gets into bed.

Can a doctor help Sam?

Will pills help? No.

Pills cannot kill cold germs.

Cold germs are virus germs.

(You say it like this: VI-rus.)

am and Benny

Sam - 3 years old
with chicken pox

Virus germs also cause the flu
and chicken pox.
Only Sam's body can kill a virus.

So what <u>can</u> Sam do?

He can get lots of sleep.

He can eat
good foods.

He can drink
lots of water

and orange juice.

These are treats
for Sam's body.

Now it's a few days later.

Sam sings in music class.

His throat does not hurt.

He plays hard.

He does not feel sick.

Sam's body
has beaten the cold germs.

He has beaten them for good.

Sam can never get sick
from the same germs again.

Does that mean
Sam will never get
another cold?
No.
There are over 200 kinds
of cold germs.
But as Sam gets older
he will get fewer colds.
Now Sam gets about
four colds a year.
His big sister gets three.
Mom and Dad get two.
Grandma only gets one.

Mom knows that the family
can catch Sam's cold.
She gives Sam
his own cup,
and his own towel,
and his own toothpaste.

This is so his family
will not pick up his cold germs.
Sometimes it works.
And sometimes . . .

. . . it doesn't.